SCRIPT

Sandy Simmons

☆ SWEET SUCCESS ☆

Jean Ure

Illustrated by Peter Kavanagh

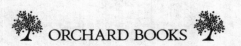
ORCHARD BOOKS

For Debbie with
even more love
P.K.

ORCHARD BOOKS
96 Leonard Street, London EC2A 4RH
Orchard Books Australia
14 Mars Road, Lane Cove, NSW 2066
First published in Great Britain in 1999
First paperback edition 1999
Text © Jean Ure 1999
Illustrations © Peter Kavanagh 1999
The rights of Jean Ure to be identified as the author
and Peter Kavanagh as the illustrator of this work
have been asserted by them in accordance with the
Copyright, Designs and Patents Act, 1988.
A CIP catalogue record for this book
is available from the British Library.
1 86039 566 X (hbk)
1 84121 017 X (pbk)
Printed in Great Britain

SANDY SIMMONS

CONTENTS

Chapter one

"It's ages since we've been sent for an audition," grumbled Rosa as we were changing into our leotards one afternoon, ready for Movement Class with Miss Merchant. "Ages and ages... Not since Christmas!"

Rosa is one of my friends at the Starlight Stage School. The school is in London and we have a special badge that is stitched on to our leotards and sweat-shirts and the bright red cloaks that we wear in winter.

Our sworn enemies from the Mona West Academy jeer at our cloaks. They call us the Red Riding Hoods. But we don't care! Cloaks are different, and we're different, too. The Monas wear puke yellow that looks like dog sick.

My other friends besides Rosa are Sasha and Dell. Sasha is my special friend. We are Sasha and Sand. Or sometimes Sandy and Sash. "Like a double act," my brother, Thomas, says.

But we are not at all alike! Sasha is pink and pretty and just a teensy tiny weeny little bit plump. Nicely Plump!

I am small and freckled with short brown hair cut sort of raggedy.

Mum says it suits me that way as I have a funny cheeky-looking face. "Like a pixie," she says. Prettyish, but not at all beautiful. Dell is the beautiful one! Rosa is what Mum calls "a chirpy Cockney sparrow" and is even smaller than I am. We all go round together in a gang.

I was surprised when Rosa grumbled about us not being sent for auditions.

"Do we expect to be?" I said. I'd only been at Starlight for one term, so I wasn't sure.

"They send the Monas," said Rosa. "They go for auditions all the time."

"Oh, well! That lot." Sasha pulled her long blond hair back into a scrunchy. "They're only interested in making money."

"I wouldn't mind making money," said Rosa.

"We will," promised Sash. "As soon as we're a bit older! They'll send us for heaps of things when we're a bit older! It doesn't do to start too young. That's what my mum says."

Sasha's mum is an actress, so she ought to know. But Starlotta, of course, couldn't resist boasting.

"I was appearing in commercials when I was only two years old. I was in an ad for diapers."

"Pardon me?" said Dell. She cupped a hand to her ear. "An ad for what, did you say?"

"Diapers," said Starlotta, in lofty tones.

There was a silence, and then I realised what she meant.

"Nappies!" I cried. "Diapers is American for nappies!"

Starlotta in a nappy ad! Everyone just collapsed.

"Oh! What did you have to do?" gasped Sasha. "Lie there on a table while your mummy changed you?"

"I crawled about," said Starlotta.

That just made us giggle even worse. I fell to my knees and started crawling, and soon all the rest had joined in. We crawled to

and fro across the changing room,
making baby noises.

"Goo gah gah!"
went Sash.

"Boo hoo! I've
wet my nappy!"
announced Rosa.

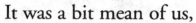

It was a bit mean of us,
I suppose, but Starlotta asks for it. She is
always making like she's so much better
than the rest of us. It's probably something
to do with having such an idiotic name
I mean, Starlotta!!! I ask you!!! I bet her
mum called her that hoping that everyone
would shorten it to Star. Nobody ever does,
though, 'cos nobody likes her. Only her
dreary friend Tiffany, who is so mindless it
is just unbelievable.

The bell rang and we all headed for the

dance studio, where Miss Merchant was waiting for us. Me and Rosa were still crawling and making baby noises.

Miss Merchant said, "On your feet, you two! We'll start with some voice exercises. Deep breath! Hold…one, two…slowly, slowly, let it out…slowly, Starlotta…and another one! Hold, one, two –"

"This is so boring," muttered Starlotta.

Well! Voice exercises might not be the most exciting thing we do but that was a really dumb thing to say. Miss Merchant kind of, like, frrrrrroze.

"Really?" she said in this icicle voice. "So you find it boring, do you?"

"Well! I mean" – Starlotta waved a hand – "I don't see the point of it."

"The point, my dear Starlotta," said Miss Merchant, "is to teach you control of your voice. How to speak without running out of breath. How to **PROJECT!**" Miss Merchant suddenly opened up and practically deafened us! "You want to be **HEARD**, don't you? There's nothing worse than sitting in a theatre and not being able to **HEAR**."

"I'm not going into theatre," declared Starlotta. Honestly! The things she says. "Theatre's way past its sell-by date. I'm only going to do films and telly."

Miss Merchant gave a short, amused laugh.

"When you're out in the big wide world, my girl, you'll do whatever's offered. Jobs don't exactly hang off the trees, you know!"

"My uncle –" began Starlotta; but everybody groaned.

Starlotta goes on and on about her uncle. He's this big telly star and he looks like a warthog. He is probably quite nice, really, but we all just get sick to death of hearing about him.

Anyway, Miss Merchant said rather crushingly that she didn't wish to know about Starlotta's uncle just at the moment.

"Here in this room I don't care what famous relatives you have. I judge you on what I see, not on who your mum and dad or auntie and uncle happen to be."

Ha! That put Starlotta in her place.

But after class, when the four of us were walking up the road together, Rosa said something that worried me. She said, "It's all very well Miss Merchant saying what she did. Not caring if someone has famous relatives. But it does help if you have one."

She meant Starlotta's gross warthoggy old uncle.

"I mean, it stands to reason," said Rosa, "doesn't it?"

"Yeah." Dell nodded, and her shiny black hair bobbed and bounced. "You got a famous uncle on the telly, he could get you a part, no problem. Just got to ask."

Dell didn't sound in the least bit bitter, but then Dell never does. She's so beautiful, she doesn't have to. She's not in the least vain about it, no way! But it has given her this massive

about a thousand metres high.

I wish I had as much confidence as Dell!

I wish I had an uncle that was a telly star.

I wish I had a mum that was an actress.

All I have is **AMBITION**.

I am going to work as hard as I can and never, ever give up. And in the end I will become a

But you can't become a star unless you are given the chance to show how brilliant you are. Rosa was right! It was time we were sent to another audition.

Chapter two

Next day, I could hardly believe it. A group of us were called in to see Miss Todd, our drama teacher, and she told us that we were being sent for – an audition!

Rosa looked at me and giggled, and I giggled back. Miss Todd said, "What is so funny, you girls? Going for auditions is a serious business."

We couldn't really tell her what we were giggling about! Rosa gave a little hiccup and

clamped a hand to her mouth. I said,
"We're excited!"

Miss Todd smiled. "It is exciting, I agree.
We don't expect you all to get parts, but it
will do you good to have a go. It's all
experience."

She said that the audition
was for a TV commercial for
a new brand of sweet called
Frooties.

"The idea is that they have lots of you
dressed up as fruits – strawberries,
raspberries, blackcurrants – all sorts! But
remember," said Miss Todd, "auditioning
for a commercial is not the same as
auditioning for a part in a play. They don't
necessarily expect you to act. What they're
mainly looking for is faces. So don't be
upset if they don't pick you. It just means

that on this occasion you weren't the type they were after."

"She only said that to make people feel better," said Starlotta later. "Anyone who really stands out" – she did a little twirl – "will always be noticed."

"Get her," muttered Rosa.

"She didn't say *she'd* stand out," said Tiffany.

But we all knew that was what she meant. Talk about a blabbermouth!

"You've got to admit," said Sash, "she's got some nerve. Just imagine how everyone will jeer if she doesn't get a part!"

"I jolly well hope she doesn't," said Rosa. "She gets right on my nerves!"

I think I got on Thomas's nerves when I got home that evening.

"Mum, Mum!" I yelled. "We've got an audition!"

Thomas groaned. "Not again!"

I said, "What do you mean, not again? The last audition I went to was before Christmas."

"Yes," said Thomas, "and we all had to suffer. Oh, I shall just DIE" – he clasped his hands to his heart – "if I don't get anything!"

"That was different," I said. "That was for a real proper show. This is just a commercial."

"Oh. I see." Thomas nodded in that

horrid superior way that he has. "Just something vulgar, to make money. Not art."

"It's all experience," I said. "But they're only looking for faces so it won't be my fault if they don't pick me. It'll just mean they don't want my particular sort of face."

"Who would?" jeered Thomas.

Thomas is always doing what he calls 'taking me down a peg'. Squashing me. He says it is necessary to stop me becoming bumptious. Mostly, I don't take any notice of him. He's terribly serious-minded. He reckons acting is a frivolous occupation.

Mum wanted to know what the commercial was for, so I told her that it was for Frooties, and that they were going to have people dressed as different kinds of fruits.

"What on earth for?" said Thomas.

I said, "I don't know. How should I know? Maybe they'll want us to do little fruit dances!" And I skipped off across the room doing a strawberry dance. Bounce – squish – bish – squash! Bounce – squish—

"She's off again," said Thomas.

"I've got to practise! Look! What's this one?"

Hop – skip – twizzle— spring. Hop – skip—

"Brussel sprout," said Thomas.

"Brussel sprout's not a fruit! I'm being a cherry!"

Hop – skip—

"I thought you said they only wanted faces?"

"Yes, but I'm getting into the mood. How do you think a banana would dance?"

"I shouldn't think they'd have a banana," said Mum.

"So what would they have?"

"Mm…peach? Passion fruit?"

"Passion fruit!" I snatched up Sheba, who is one of our cats, and began to cover her in kisses. "Mwah! Mwah! Mwah!" Then I whirled off across the room, clutching her to me.

Thomas made a being-sick noise. "Mum, does she have to?" he said.

Mum just laughed and told him to stop being a misery.

"Of course," sighed Thomas, "I have to remember that she is still very young."

Honestly! You'd think Thomas was about ninety the way he carries on. He is only a year older than me!

Chapter three

The audition was held the very next day. We all travelled on the tube to Leicester Square, and Miss Todd came with us. The people who were making the commercial were called Fogel, Fitch & Fairlie Walker, which for some reason made me and Rosa go off into one of our fits of giggles. We kept chanting it as we sat on the tube: "Fogel, *Fitch* and Fairlie Walker!"

In the end Miss Todd had to tell us to be quiet and stop showing off. She said she was ashamed to be seen with us.

"Just behave yourselves! You'll give the school a bad name."

After that we sat as quiet as mice and didn't look at each other. We knew that if we looked we'd only start off giggling again.

"It's just so unprofessional," grumbled Starlotta.

Fogel Fitch lived right at the top of a skyscraper building made of shiny green glass, like something out of a fairy tale. We sailed up to the sixteenth floor in a lift that had mirrors all round it. I couldn't help shooting little anxious glances at myself and wondering whether I had the sort of face that they were  looking for. Yes, and I wasn't the only one! I caught Starlotta doing it, as well.

The lift glided to a halt and we all trooped out and walked along a corridor covered in thick white carpet. One of the boys jabbed at Rosa and whispered, "Hey! You'd better watch out! This carpet's so thick a little thing like you could get lost in it."

Rosa biffed at him and Miss Todd said, "Sh! That's enough of that."

They're very strict at Starlight. They don't like you doing anything that might give the school a bad name.

At the end of the corridor was a glass door with the word RECEPTION printed on it. Miss Todd went through, and we followed. And, oh, help! The room was full of Monas! Dozens of them, sitting there in their yucky yellow uniforms, all smug and self-satisfied 'cos they'd got there first.

We had to stand.

One of the Monas was a girl called Janis
that I recognised from the Christmas show
we'd been in. Janis wasn't too bad, for a
Mona. She came over to me and Rosa and
said, "It's all right, we've already been in.
We're just waiting for Susie."

"What was it like?" said Rosa.

Janis shrugged. "Oh! You know. Same as
always."

Rosa nodded wisely. I waited till the
Monas had gone swaggering off with their
teacher then whispered, "What did she
mean, same as always?"

"I dunno," said Rosa.

Rosa is so cool! She wasn't going to let on
to a Mona that she'd never been for a
commercial before. Whatever you do, you
can't afford to let them think they're
superior. They already crow quite enough

as it is, just because their school is nearer the West End than ours.

While we were waiting to be called in, a man came out and took our photographs with a Polaroid camera. I asked if I could have a look at mine, just to make sure I hadn't come out like a squashed toad or a lump of mashed potato, which is the sort of thing that can happen if the camera catches you at the wrong moment. The man didn't seem to mind, but Starlotta rolled her

SANDY SIMMONS

eyes and mouthed, "Un-pro-FESSION-al."

I didn't see why it was. If I'd come out like

a mashed potato I would have asked him to take another one. But, anyway, I looked OK apart from my ears sticking out, but there's nothing I can do about that. I've tried using chewing gum and I've tried using Sellotape and just nothing seems to work. Mum says I'm over-sensitive and that nobody else even notices.

But if you want to be a ★S★T★A★R★ you have to be aware of these things.

A woman with long silver fingernails and slinky black trousers checked off our names on a list. One by one we were called in. I was glad Miss Todd had put my name as Sandy and not Alexandra. I can't bear being called Alexandra! Alexandra Simmons. Ugh! But as my surname begins with an S, I am always one of the last to be called.

Rosa is lucky as she is Rosa Carmirelli.

And Dell is Della Dugard. Even Sash is Sasha McGowran, which isn't too bad. They all went in before me! I just had to sit there and try not to chew my nails, which is a stupid habit that I've got.

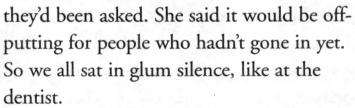

Miss Todd wouldn't let anyone say what it was like, or tell what questions they'd been asked. She said it would be off-putting for people who hadn't gone in yet. So we all sat in glum silence, like at the dentist.

"You can talk, you know," said Miss Todd. "I didn't say don't talk! I just said don't discuss."

But nobody could think of anything to

talk about! Starlotta, trying to show how terribly professional she was, picked up a magazine and pretended to read it. I knew she was only pretending when I looked over her shoulder and saw that it was all in a foreign language!

Her name comes just before mine: Starlotta Sharman. I almost tore off a whole fingernail while I was waiting for her to come out. I just couldn't help it. I'd told Thomas that a commercial wasn't the same as a real proper show, and of course it isn't. But I still most desperately wanted to be picked!

I prayed inside my head, over and over: Please, let them be looking for someone like me! A freckle-faced pixie with sticking-out ears – it didn't seem very likely! But as Sasha is fond of saying, you never know your luck.

Starlotta came out with this big smirking smile on her face. I could just feel her looking at my freckles and my ears and thinking, "She doesn't stand a chance!"

But I took a deep breath and went marching in. The room was absolutely mega-normous. One whole wall was nothing but window! All dotted about were these very low, glass-topped tables and white spindly chairs. Long green trailing things were growing out of pots and huge monster fans hung from the ceiling like giant spiders. Really creepy!

At the far end of the room there was a man in a red shirt sitting at a table. Behind him there were three more men and a girl in a sparkly top. They were all wearing dark glasses like gangsters in an American movie.

The man in the red shirt said, "And who have we here? Sandy, isn't it? Sandy Simmons. Hi there, Sandy! I'm Steve. These are Mike, Pete, Andy and Jill... Mike, Pete, Andy, Jill, meet Sandy."

Everyone said "Hi", so I said "Hi" back.

They laughed when I said it. I don't know why. I was only being polite.

On my way across the room I bumped into a table and got tangled up with one of the trailing things and they all laughed again. I felt really stupid. I bet Starlotta hadn't got tangled in a trailing thing!

Steve said, "OK, Sandy! This is a commercial for Frooties, as I expect you know. Here's the story line."

I did my best to look intelligent.

"Boy and girl in sweet shop, gazing at the sweets – yum yum! – which ones shall they buy? They can't decide! Then all of a sudden – whoosh!" He threw up his hands. "A tube of Frooties bursts open and all the fruits come spilling out – raspberries, strawberries – "

"Oranges, lemons – "

"Blackberries – "

"Mangoes – "

All the others had joined in, excitedly calling out the names of fruits.

"Does that sound fun or does that sound fun?" said Steve.

I said, "That sounds absolutely brilliant," and they all laughed yet again. I couldn't think what I'd said that was amusing. I was just trying to show them that I felt as excited as they did.

"Okey-dokey! Let's get down to business. Mike!"

One of the other men stood up and pointed a video camera at me.

"I want you to look into this camera, Sandy, and shout out the word 'Frooties!' Can you do that?"

"I should think so," I said. It didn't sound very difficult.

"You won't dry when the camera starts rolling?"

I said indignantly that of course I wouldn't! I said, "Miss Todd would be furious if any of us did that."

So then they laughed yet again. I still couldn't understand why they kept doing it, but I was getting used to it by now.

Steve said, "Right. Off you go!"

The camera light came on. I looked straight at it and shouted "FROOOOteeeze!" as loudly as I could.

The girl in the sparkly top said, "Ace!" Mike stuck up a thumb.

"OK, Sandy." Steve leaned across to shake my hand.

I blinked. Was that it?

"Thanks a bunch! Nice of you to come along."

They didn't want me! Something must have put them off. The freckles? The ears? Or was it because I'd got caught in the trailing thing?

"Please don't mention it," I said.

It was just good manners. There wasn't any reason for them to laugh.

Steve took out his handkerchief and dried his eyes.

"This one we have to use," he said. "Don't worry, Sandy! You'll be hearing from us."

Wow!

WOW!

I reeled back outside and collapsed on a chair next to Sasha. I was absolutely bursting to tell someone what Steve had said! *You'll be hearing from us…*

Had he said it to everyone? Or just to me? I couldn't wait to find out!

Chapter four

As soon as we could, we exchanged notes.

"And then I had to shout 'Frooties!'" said Sasha, "straight into the camera."

"Yeah." Dell nodded. "Me, too."

"Yes, I did that," agreed Rosa.

"Same here."

"And me!"

It turned out we'd all had to shout "Frooties!"

"He asked me if I'd dry when the camera started rolling."

"Yes, he asked me that!"

He'd asked everyone the same question.

"What did you say?"

Sasha giggled. "I said I hoped not!"

"I said Miss Todd would be furious with us if we did anything like that."

"You didn't?" Starlotta spun round accusingly.

"Yes, I did." I tilted my head. "And he laughed."

"So *unprofessional*," hissed Starlotta.

"Unprofessional," tittered Tiffany.

I turned my back on them and went stalking off ahead with Sash and the others. We were walking to the tube station, a great gaggle of us. We weren't supposed to walk in gaggles. Miss Todd said it cluttered the pavement and gave the school a bad name.

"What did he say right at the end?" I asked Sasha.

"Oh, just…thank you for coming and we'll be in touch."

"That's what they always say!" yelled Starlotta. "It just means they haven't yet made up their minds. They say it to everyone."

"Did he say it to you?" said Sasha. "Oy!" She poked at me. "Did he say it to you?"

"N-no. He said –"

"What? What did he say?"

"He said, 'This one we have to use.' And then he said, 'Don't worry, you'll be hearing from us.'"

There was a stunned silence.

"He said *what*?" said Dell.

"He said, 'Don't worry, you'll be hearing from us'…"

"And, 'This one we have to use.'?"

"Yes."

"Jumping Geronimo!"

"You've got a part!" said Sash.

Starlotta, for once, didn't say anything at all.

When I got home I hurled myself into the kitchen shouting, "Mum, Mum, I've got a part!"

"Oh, that's wonderful!" cried Mum. "What part is it?"

"And how much are they paying?" said Thomas.

I had to admit that I hadn't yet been told which part it was. Only that I'd got one!

"But what about the money?" roared Thomas.

Mum said, "Oh, Thomas, as if the money matters! It's the honour and glory."

"Is it?" said Thomas. "I thought it was the money."

"Who cares about money? Not me!"

I went dancing off round the kitchen doing my strawberry dance. Bounce – squish – bish – squash! I felt sure that I would be picked as a strawberry.

As soon as Dad got in, Mum told him the news.

"Sandy's going to be a big star! She's got a part in a commercial!"

"This is excellent," said Dad, rubbing his hands. "If she carries on like this I'll be able to retire!" And then, like Mum, he wanted to know what part it was.

"She doesn't know," said Thomas. "She doesn't even know what they're paying!"

I explained that they had promised I would be hearing from them. I told Dad how Steve had said, "This one we have to use."

"Well, let's hope he's as good as his word," said Dad. "I don't think we ought to start celebrating until it's actually in the bag."

"Bag?" I said. "What bag?"

"He means, until the contract's signed," said Mum.

"Oh!" I wasn't terribly interested in contracts. I just wanted to know what part I'd got!

On the tube next morning with Sash I said, "I should think I'd be a strawberry, wouldn't you? I have a strawberryish sort of face."

"Well, you said it," said Sash.

"Oh, I don't mind," I assured her. "I'd sooner be a strawberry than a raspberry. I don't like raspberries. But, of course, I'll be whatever they want me to be."

"Don't have much choice, really," muttered Sasha.

As we left the tube station we met up with some of the others. Dell and Rosa, Tiffany, Starlotta.

"Well?" said Starlotta. She smiled at me sweetly. "Have you heard yet?"

"Not yet," I said.

"Oh, I am surprised! I thought they'd have sent you a telegram."

"They wouldn't get in touch with Sandy," said Dell. "They'd get in touch with the school."

"Oh well! He's probably on the telephone right now. They obviously didn't want anyone too pretty." Starlotta explained to Tiffany.

"If they had, they'd have chosen you," gushed Tiffany.

Ugh! She is so yucky.

"Please don't get on my case," I said. I did my little strawberry dance along the pavement. Bounce – squish – bish – squash! "I can't help it if he gives me a part."

"Sandy, what exactly are you doing?" said Rosa, as I strawberried past her and almost knocked an old lady into the gutter.

"I'm being a strawberry!'"

"Ha!" said Starlotta. "So that's what he was looking for!"

And she immediately began to copy my strawberry dance, except that she did it with puffed-out cheeks and bent knees and her bottom stuck up in  the air. Flump – bump – plish – plosh.

"Squashed strawberry!"

Everyone giggled, even Sasha.

I didn't care! They were just jealous. All of them.

"You know what you'll be," I said to Starlotta, "if you get a part – you'll be a *gooseberry!*"

I puckered my mouth as if I was eating lemons and I held my arms very stiff and straight at my sides and I did a bright green gooseberry dance right in front of her, all thin and mean and mimsy.

"Sour goosegog!" I cried. "That's what you'll be!"

Later that day Mrs Lovejoy, the school secretary, came into our classroom and said that Miss Todd wanted to see the following people in her office immediately before lunch: "Della Dugard, Sasha McGowran,

Starlotta Sharman and Barry Brown."

Rosa shot a look at me.
I smiled brightly. I wasn't
worried! Steve had
promised. "You'll be
hearing from us…"

The minute the bell
rang, the four of them went
dashing off, helter-skelter, for Miss Todd's
office. They weren't supposed to run in the
corridor, but nobody stopped them.

"Well," said Rosa. "It's very odd. If he
promised."

"It's probably about something quite
different," I said.

But, oh, it wasn't! When they came back,
they were all happy and beaming. They
had all got parts in the Frootie ad! Dell
was a passion fruit, Sash was a peach,

Barry was a mango. And Starlotta –
Starlotta was a strawberry.

Chapter five

Just for a minute, I felt I was going to be sick all over the lunch table. My tummy ballooned right up into my mouth, my hands went all wet and sticky and my knife and fork started to shake and make tinkly noises on my plate.

And then Sasha said, "By the way, Sand, Miss Todd wants to see you as soon as you've finished lunch."

"About what?" I said, twiddling my fork in my pasta and trying to make like I

couldn't have cared less.

"I don't know. She didn't say. She just said to tell you."

"Oh! Well. I'm going to finish my lunch first," I said.

"That's what she said," said Sasha. "There isn't any hurry."

"It's obviously nothing important," I said.

All the same, there was one little bit of me that couldn't help hoping... Maybe they had rung about me specially, and that was why she wanted to see me on my own.

"We were extremely impressed with little Sandy Simmons!"

I forced myself to eat my plate of pasta, even though it kept clogging up my mouth so I could hardly swallow it. I even ate my yoghurt, which I had chosen on purpose because it was strawberry. I hoped nobody

would notice, but of course old beady-eyed
Tiffany did.

"Oh, look, Star!" She pointed.
"She's eating your yoghurt!"

I felt like throwing it at her.

As soon as I'd finished I
raced off to Miss Todd's
office. One of the
teachers saw me and
yelled "Sandy Simmons!
You know you're not
supposed to be running
in the corridor!"

Nobody had told the others
not to run.

Miss Todd was waiting for me. She smiled
as I came in, but it wasn't the sort of smile
that meant she was going to give me good
news. It was more of a – a *kind* sort of

smile. A try-to-be-ever-so-brave sort of smile.

I found that I'd started shaking again.

Miss Todd said, "Sit down, Sandy!"

I sat very quickly, before my legs could give way.

"I'm so sorry," said Miss Todd, "that you weren't offered a part in the Frootie commercial."

It was just as well she'd told me to sit down or I would probably have gone crashing on to the floor. I couldn't believe it! I just couldn't believe it! He had *promised*.

Gently, Miss Todd said, "You were so sure you were going to get something, weren't you?"

"He promised me!" I cried. "He said he was going to use me!"

"Oh, Sandy." Miss Todd shook her head.
"People say a lot of things."

"You mean he – he didn't mean it?"

"He probably meant it when he said it.
While you were there, in front of him. But
then afterwards perhaps he thought about
it, or he saw someone else, or things just
didn't quite work out the way they were
supposed to... I'm afraid, in this business,
it doesn't do to count your
chickens before they're
hatched."

It was what Dad had
said. "I don't think we
ought to start
celebrating until it's
actually in the bag."

I dragged the sleeve of my sweatshirt
across my eyes. I wasn't going to cry! You

had to be tough if you
wanted to get anywhere.

"It's a hard lesson,"
said Miss Todd, "but
it's one we all have to
learn."

The worst part was
having to go back
and face the others.
After all the fuss I'd
made! Dancing my

stupid strawberry dance. Telling Starlotta she
was a sour gooseberry. How she would gloat!

She did.

"So much for squashed strawberries," she
said.

"And sour gooseberries," said Tiffany with
a little smirk.

"Fancy believing what anyone tells you!"

Starlotta gave an amused trill. "I learnt not to do that when I was two years old!"

"Sandy doesn't come from a theatrical family," said Tiffany.

"No, that's true." Starlotta stopped trilling and heaved a big sigh, making like she felt sorry for me. "Poor Sandy! She's got a lot to learn."

I now know how an insect feels when someone treads on it.

FLATTENED

I couldn't even think of anything smart to say in reply.

"You don't want to let her get to you," said Sasha, as she dragged me away. "She's not worth bothering with! She's just garbage."

"She's not even any good," I muttered.

"Well, she is quite," said Sasha. "And she had done more work than any of the rest of us."

"That doesn't give her the right to gloat!"

"No, but she's that sort of person. And if you don't mind me saying so," said Sasha, "you did rather ask for it…all that dancing around in the street! You were just lucky Miss Todd didn't catch you. You know how she feels about that sort of thing. Showing off in public," said Sasha.

I opened my mouth to say that I hadn't been showing off, I'd just been excited. But then I closed it again, because I knew that really and truly Sasha was right. I had been excited – but I'd been showing off as well.

I'd been gloating over Starlotta.

I thought when I got home and broke the

news that Thomas would gloat over *me*, but to my surprise he didn't. He was quite kind. He even tried to cheer me up.

"After all, it was only a commercial," he said. "Not a real proper show."

"That's right," said Mum. "Not worth shedding any tears over."

But I did shed tears all the same. Only I waited till I was in bed and shed them into my pillow.

There is such a thing as pride.

Chapter six

I didn't want to go to school next morning. I tried telling Mum I was feeling sick, but she didn't believe me.

She said, "Sandy, sweetheart, I know this is hard for you, but you can't just run away from things. You have to face up to them. Be brave! I'm sure it won't be anywhere near as bad as you think."

Mum didn't know Starlotta. She and Tiffany were still going to be gloating, and even some of the others might look at me and think, "Serves her right." I hadn't been boastful – I didn't *think* I'd been boastful – but I could see that maybe I might have got

on people's nerves a bit with my strawberry
dance.

Me and Sasha travelled to school together
on the tube, the same as always. But instead
of giggling and gossiping, which is what we
usually do, we were quite solemn and
serious.

"You mustn't let things get to you," said
Sash. "It happens to everybody at one time
or another."

"What? People saying they're going to use
you and then not doing it?"

"Yes! Mum says if she could have ten pence for every time she's been let down, she'd be a millionaire by now."

"I don't think people should be allowed to say things they don't mean," I muttered.

"Mum says you get used to it. She says you have to learn to take everything with a pinch of salt. It's a tough business," said Sasha. She meant show business. "You have to be tough to survive."

I was tough! But it was just so unfair. I said so to Sasha and she rolled her eyes and said, "Tell me about it!"

In the corridor at school we bumped into Starlotta. She said, "Oh, there you are, Sandy Simmons! You're in for it. Miss Todd's looking for you."

"For me?" I said.

"Well, your name is Sandy Simmons, isn't

it? She wants you in her office straight away. She looks grim! I reckon someone's gone and reported you."

"Reported her for what?" said Sasha.

"Giving the school a bad name! Dancing in the street."

"You were doing it too!" I said.

"I didn't knock an old lady into the gutter."

"Oh!" Sasha clapped a hand to her mouth. She looked at me in dismay. Giving the school a bad name is one of the worst crimes. But knocking an old lady into the gutter…

I swallowed, rather hard.

"You didn't even apologise to her," said Starlotta. "You were too busy showing off."

Sasha gave me a little shove. "You'd better go and see Miss Todd and get it over with. I'll keep my fingers crossed for you!"

I snailed along to Miss Todd's office and scratched nervously at the door. My heart was banging and thudding. What was she going to say to me?

"Sandy Simmons, you are a disgrace to the school!"

She might even expel me.

"Come in!" called Miss Todd.

I eased open the door just the tiniest little crack and sidled

through it sideways. I thought perhaps if I
was very meek and humble she might
forgive me.

"Ah, Sandy!" said Miss Todd.
She didn't *sound* grim.
She didn't look grim.
She was smiling! A
proper smile! A happy
smile!
"Take a seat, Sandy.
Good news! Fogel Fitch
just rang. They want you, after all."

I got as far as "W—" and then my mouth
just dropped into this great big O.

"Apparently," said Miss Todd, "they saw
you first, and then they saw another girl. It
was between the two of you! They couldn't
make up their minds. It's taken them all
this time! They rang through just this

morning to say they wanted you. And it's not to dress up as a Frootie, it's to play a real part – the girl in the sweet shop! Isn't that lovely?"

I tried desperately to change my lips into a different shape so that I could say something, but they seemed to have got permanently stuck on the letter O.

"It means you actually have a speaking part," said Miss Todd. "You get to say—"

My mouth suddenly sprang back into working order.

"FROOOOOteeeze!" I cried.

"Y-e-es…" Miss Todd pressed both hands to her ears. "I'm glad you've already learnt your lines!"

The others were all in the classroom waiting for registration. Sasha looked at me anxiously.

"What happened?"

I felt like jumping on to a desk and shouting, "I've got a part! I've got a speaking part!"

But I didn't. I just said in a perfectly ordinary, quiet sort of voice that the advertising agency had rung.

"They want me, after all."

"Oh! Sandy! That is brilliant!"

Sasha is so lovely. She came flying over and gave me a huge bear hug.

Starlotta said, "What do they want you for? An orange pip?"

Tiffany snickered. She thought that was really funny.

"No, I'm going to be the girl in the sweet shop," I said.

"Jumping Geronimo!" said Dell. Sasha went into a mock faint.

"That's a lead part!"

"Just think...you'll be rich," said Rosa. "You'll earn a fortune!"

I said, "It won't be a fortune. Not like winning the lottery."

"Better than a poke in the eye with a burnt stick," sighed Rosa.

I felt terrible. I'd been so busy feeling sorry for myself that I'd never bothered to think of poor Rosa. She hadn't been offered anything at all!

"It's only a commercial," I said. "Not like a real proper show. It's not going to make me into a star overnight."

"Hardly!" brayed Starlotta.

"It's the product that counts." agreed Tiffany. She nodded wisely. "It's what you said…they obviously didn't want anyone too pretty. If they had someone too pretty, it would draw attention away from the product."

The product was the most important thing in any commercial. I knew that! I knew that it was Frooties that were important and not me.

But Sasha said loyally that when people watched it, it would be my face that they remembered.

"You'll be recognised every time you walk down the street."

I'd be the Girl in the Frooties Ad!

About the Author

Jean Ure was still at school when she had her first novel published. She's written lots of books since then, including the *Woodside School* stories and, for older children, *Love is Forever*. As well as writing, Jean really LOVES drama, acting and the theatre! After finishing school, Jean went to The Webber-Douglas Academy and some of her ideas for the Sandy Simmons stories come from her experiences there. Jean now lives in Croydon with her husband, seven dogs and three cats.

SCRIPT